Ten Little

by Bill Martin Jr

Caterpillars
illustrated by Lois Ehlert

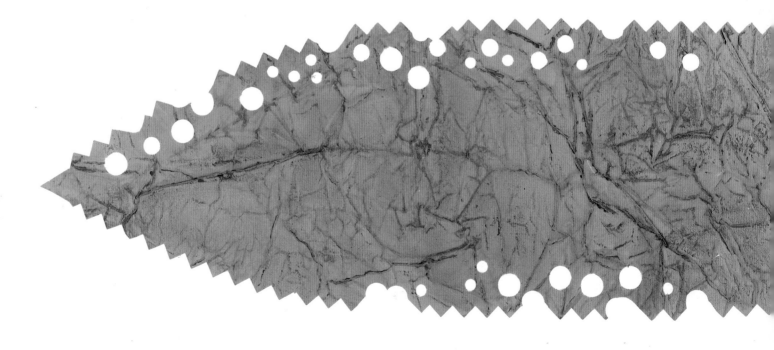

BEACH LANE BOOKS
New York • London • Toronto • Sydney

The first little caterpillar

wild rose

crawled into a bower.

The second little caterpillar

delphinium

gaillardia
(blanketflower)

wriggled up a flower.

foxglove

snapdragon

The third little caterpillar

cabbage

climbed a cabbage head.

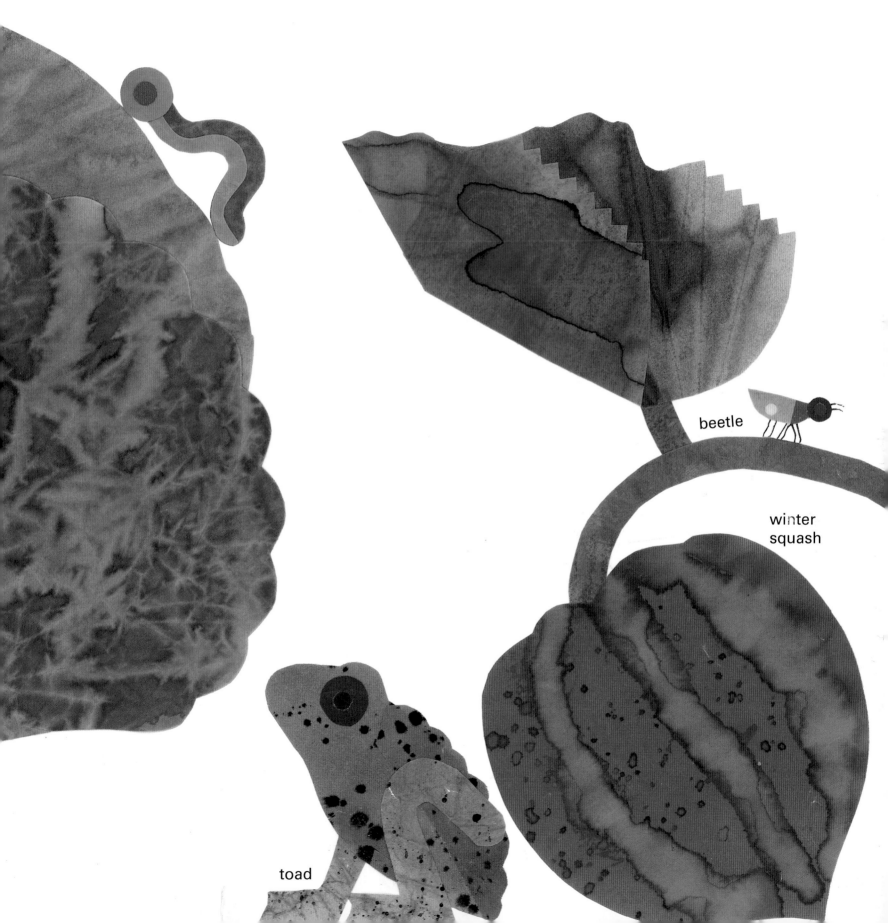

beetle

winter
squash

toad

The fourth little caterpillar

watermelon

found a melon bed.

The fifth little caterpillar

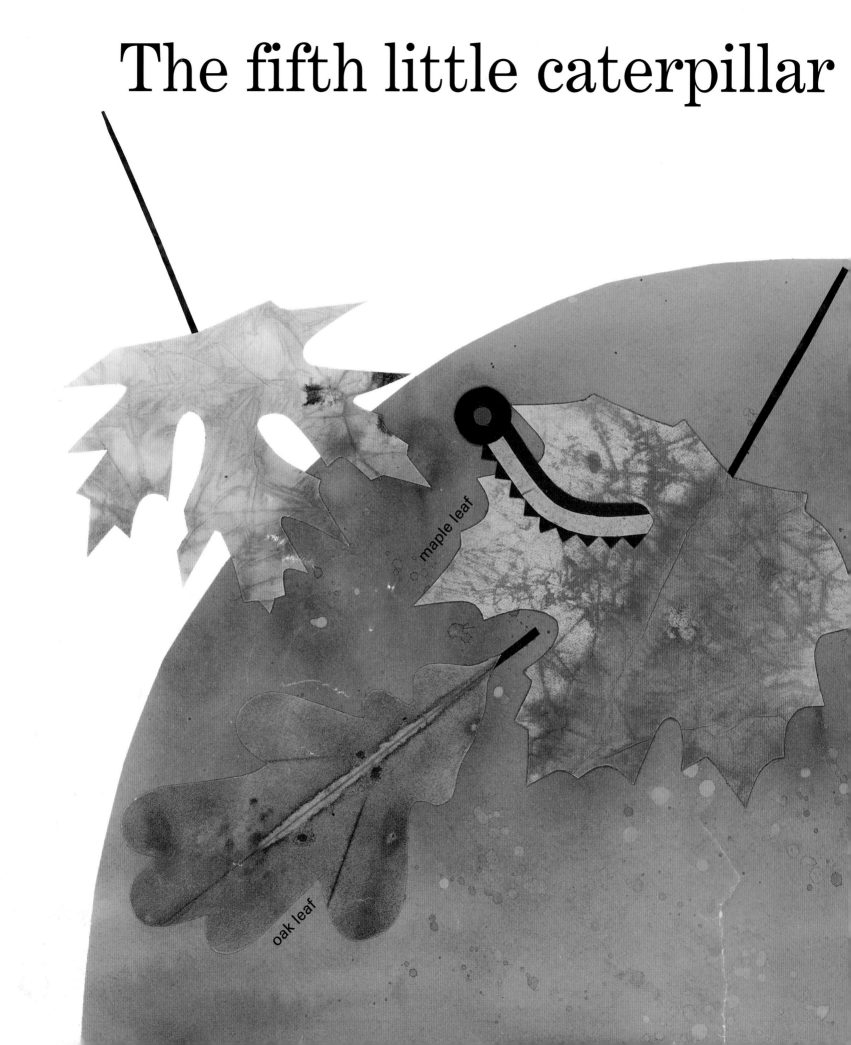

maple leaf

oak leaf

sailed a garden pool.

poplar leaf

The sixth little caterpillar

spider

jar

was carried off to school.

monarch eggs

monarch chrysalis

milkweed plant

The seventh little caterpillar

thistle plant

dragonfly

met a hungry wren.

grasshopper

The eighth little caterpillar

winter
squash

was frightened by a hen.

The ninth little caterpillar

sea bass

fell into the sea.

The tenth little caterpillar

apple tree branch

apple

scaled an apple tree . . .

leaf

and hung there patiently . . .

tiger swallowtail
chrysalis

cardinal

until by and by,

apple
blossoms

the tenth little caterpillar . . .

bee

became a butterfly.

buddleia (butterfly bush)

1

mourning cloak

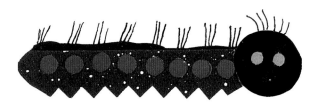

caterpillar
Feeds on tree leaves,
nettles, and wild rose leaves

butterfly

2

buckeye

caterpillar
Feeds on a variety
of leaves, including
snapdragon leaves

butterfly

3

cabbage looper

caterpillar

Devours leaves;
likes garden crops

moth

4

yellow bear

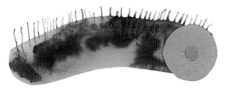

caterpillar

Chomps on
tree leaves and
leaves of garden crops

Virginian tiger
moth

5

yellow-necked

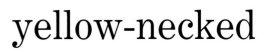

caterpillar

Feeds on tree leaves

moth

6

monarch

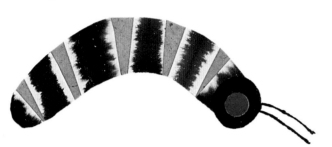

caterpillar
Eats only milkweed leaves

butterfly

7

painted lady

caterpillar
Feeds on thistle leaves
and other plants such as daisies

butterfly

8

woolly bear

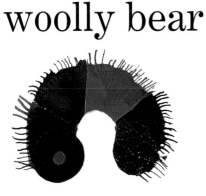

caterpillar

Eats many low-growing plants,
grasses, and weeds

Isabella tiger
moth

9

common wood nymph

caterpillar

Feeds on grasses
in woods, meadows, and fields

butterfly

10

tiger swallowtail

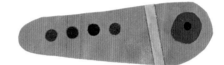

caterpillar

Eats shrub and broadleaf tree leaves

butterfly